W9-CTF-112

DATE DUE

MR 06 '00	JAN 3 1 2008	2008 3 9
APR 08 2008		2008 3 6
		APR 15 2008
	FEB 1 4 2008	
	FEB 1 2 2008	

DEMCO 38-297

BIRDS

JEN GREEN

Gareth Stevens Publishing
MILWAUKEE

For Hannah, Edward, and Stephen

The original publishers would like to thank their models: Jeffrey Adams, Maria Bloodworth,
David Callega, Ricky Garret, Ella Goldstein, Jeff Green, Stella Rae James, Roxanne John,
Canan Kaya, Alexander Morallo, Ifunanya Obi, and Shazea Rahman. They also thank: Bristol
Zoo, Education Centre; City Museum and Art Gallery, Bristol; The World Parrot Trust,
Cornwall. Special thanks to Papilio Photography for all their patient and efficient help.

**For a free color catalog describing Gareth Stevens' list of high-quality books
and multimedia programs, call 1-800-542-2595 (USA) or 1-800-461-9120
(Canada). Gareth Stevens Publishing's Fax: (414) 225-0377.
See our catalog, too, on the World Wide Web: http://gsinc.com**

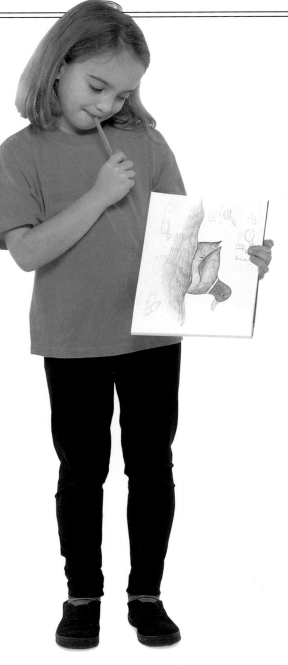

Library of Congress Cataloging-in-Publication Data

Green, Jen.
Birds / by Jen Green. — North American ed.
p. cm. — (Young scientist concepts and projects)
Includes bibliographical references and index.
Summary: Describes a variety of birds as they hatch, find a mate,
build their nests, and migrate. Includes projects such as making a
nesting box and identifying food remains.
ISBN 0-8368-2161-0 (lib. bdg.)
1. Birds—Juvenile literature.   2. Birds—Experiments—Juvenile literature.
[1. Birds.]   I. Title.   II. Series: Young scientist concepts and projects.
QL676.2.G73   1998
598—dc21   98-13700

This North American Edition first published in 1998 by
Gareth Stevens Publishing
1555 North RiverCenter Drive, Suite 201
Milwaukee, WI 53212 USA

Original edition © 1998 by Anness Publishing Limited.
First published in 1998 by Lorenz Books, an imprint of
Anness Publishing Inc., New York, New York.
This U.S. edition © 1998 by Gareth Stevens, Inc.
Additional end matter © 1998 by Gareth Stevens, Inc.

Editor: Ann Kay
Consultant: David Burnie
Photographer: John Freeman
Stylist: Melanie Williams
Designer: Ann Samuel
Picture researcher: Liz Eddison
Illustrator: Cy Baker/Wildlife Art
Gareth Stevens series editor: Dorothy L. Gibbs
Editorial assistant: Diane Laska

Printed in the United States of America

1 2 3 4 5 6 7 8 9 02 01 00 99 98

BIRDS

CONTENTS

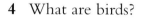

WHAT ARE BIRDS?

The black-browed albatross has a huge wingspan. Its relative, the wandering albatross, has the largest wingspan of all birds — up to 11 feet (3.4 m). These large, heavy seabirds spend their lives flying over the world's great oceans. Most come on land only to breed.

BIRDS are warm-blooded animals, like mammals, but they lay eggs, like reptiles and amphibians. Unlike other animals, birds' bodies are covered with strong, lightweight feathers. Feathers help birds fly, although there are a few birds that cannot fly. Because most birds can fly, they are equally at home in the air and on land. Birds live all across the world, on all seven continents from Africa to Antarctica. They inhabit icy polar regions, tropical rain forests, and scorching deserts. They are found in crowded cities, as well as on high mountains and remote islands. Birds vary greatly in size. The tiny bee hummingbird of Cuba is no larger than a bumblebee. The African ostrich, at the other extreme, stands 8 feet (2.4 meters) high.

Body shape

Look closely at the body shape of this American robin. All birds have this basic body shape, but they vary greatly in size and color. All birds also have a beak, instead of jaws with teeth, and they have scaly legs and feet. Flying birds have powerful wings and a feathered tail, to help them balance. Although American and European robins both have bright red breasts, the American robin is actually a kind of thrush.

Nostril
Crown
Beak (bill)
Nape
Throat
Breast
Back
Wing
Rump
Belly
Claw
Flank
Tail

4

Feathers

A great egret (*left*) is busy cleaning its feathers, or preening. The bodies of most birds are covered with feathers, except on the legs and beak. Feathers protect a bird's body and keep it warm. The color of a bird's feathers, or plumage, can help it hide from enemies or attract a mate.

All feathers have a similar shape, but they come in many colors.

Laying eggs

Instead of giving birth to babies, as most mammals do, birds lay eggs. Many birds lay their eggs in nests to shelter them. They sit on the eggs to keep them warm while the baby birds develop inside. As a baby bird grows, the egg's hard shell protects it, and the egg's yolk nourishes it.

The first bird

The earliest birdlike creature known to science is the *Archaeopteryx*. Fossils of these animals (*above*) have been found in Germany, preserved in rocks. This prehistoric ancestor of modern birds lived about 150 million years ago. It had a reptilelike head, sharp teeth, a long tail, and feathered wings. *Archaeopteryx* could not fly well, but it could glide down from high perches.

BIRD-WATCHING

BIRDS are everywhere, in the city and in the country. Because many of them have colorful feathers, they are among the easiest animals to spot. You can observe some kinds of birds from your home or from your school classroom, but, to see a wider range of species, you will need to go out bird-watching. Most bird-watchers have a certain place they visit regularly to look for birds. It might be a local park, a pond, or a woods. Never go bird-watching alone, and always tell an adult where you are going. Birds are shy creatures, so they use their keen eyesight and good hearing to stay on the lookout for enemies. The best way to observe them is to be very quiet and still.

Take cover
Always approach birds quietly and, if possible, stay at least partially hidden so you do not frighten them away. Try out different kinds of cover to see how well each kind works. For example, watch from behind a bush or a tree, or even a parked car.

Bird-watching equipment
Among the things you will need for watching birds, a notebook is the most important item. Your clothes should be a dull color, and be sure to dress warmly in cold weather. Take along a waterproof mat to keep you dry and warm on damp ground.

Waterproof mat

Boots or outdoor shoes

Notebook

Lightweight binoculars

Warm hat

Scarf

Gloves or mittens

Field guide (with clear pictures of the birds in your area)

Pens or pencils

Colored pencils or crayons

Using binoculars

1 Lightweight binoculars are very useful on bird-watching trips. Remove them from the case and hang them around your neck so they are ready to use.

2 When you spot a bird, do not look down or you might lose sight of it. Keep watching it while you slowly raise the binoculars to your eyes. Avoid sudden movements.

3 Adjust the focusing wheel on your binoculars to bring the bird into focus. Focusing might be difficult at first, but it will get easier with practice.

Drawing birds

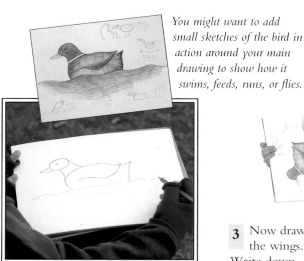

You might want to add small sketches of the bird in action around your main drawing to show how it swims, feeds, runs, or flies.

1 You do not have to be an artist to draw birds. Study the shape of the bird and notice how long the neck is. Start by drawing simple ovals for the head and body.

2 Look at the shape and size of the bird's beak. Look at its neck and tail. If you can see its legs, how long are they? Can you see its feet? Add these details to your drawing.

3 Now draw the wings. Write down some notes about the bird's coloring, so you can color your drawing later.

FAMILIES AND SHAPES

Scientists have divided birds into 27 groups, called orders. The orders are divided into 155 smaller groups, called families. Still smaller groups, called species, include birds closely related to each other. Birds of a species have similar body shapes and can mate with each other. The shape of a bird's body makes it suited to a certain way of life. For example, a duck has a wide body and webbed feet to help it move through the water. There are more than 8,600 different species of birds in the world. The largest order of birds is the perching birds, those with feet designed for perching. This order includes 5,110 different species. The basic body shapes of five major bird families are shown on the next page.

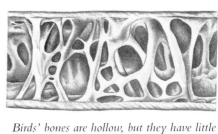

Birds' bones are hollow, but they have little bony supports inside to strengthen them (see drawing above). The skeletons of flying birds are very light to save on the amount of weight they have to carry in the air.

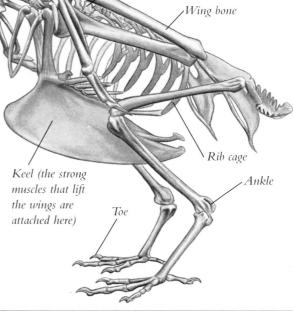

Skull

Nostril

Neck

Backbone

Wing bone

Rib cage

Ankle

Keel (the strong muscles that lift the wings are attached here)

Toe

FACT BOX

• The ostrich is an unusual bird. It is the only species in its family.

• Larger bird species often live the longest. Giant albatrosses can live for eighty years.

• Small songbird species, such as sparrows and chickadees, often live for only one year.

Bird skeleton
A bird's skeleton has a shape designed for flight, with wings instead of front limbs. Wings and legs are the heaviest parts of a bird's body. They are arranged close to the center of the body to help the bird balance.

Long-legged waders
Herons live in lakes, streams, and marshes. They have very long legs that are ideal for wading in the shallow water where they hunt for prey. Their long, flexible necks allow them to jab at prey, such as fish and frogs, with lightning speed.

Small but adaptable
Finches belong to the songbird family. Songbirds are small, lightweight birds that live on land. They hop rather than walk along the ground. Songbirds can be found on every continent except Antarctica.

An aquatic life
Swans are found around freshwater streams and ponds. They have broad bodies and webbed feet, ideal shapes for living on water. Their long, graceful necks let them dip their heads underwater to search for food.

Soaring hunters
Eagles are large birds of prey. They have powerful wings that make them able to fly great distances in search of food. Eagles have sharp vision, so they can hunt small animals such as rabbits, snakes, lizards, and fish.

Animal trackers
Owls are predators that eat small animals, such as mice. Their compact shape and broad wings make them well-suited for swooping down on their prey. Owls sleep during the day and hunt at night.

BEAKS AND FEEDING

A bird's beak, or bill, is a very useful, all-purpose tool. Birds use their beaks to catch and hold onto their food, and, sometimes, to prepare the food for eating. Different kinds of birds feed on a wide variety of foods. Some eat seeds and other types of plant matter. Other birds feed on insects, worms, and snails. Birds of prey hunt small mammals, such as mice and rabbits. Many waterbirds eat fish, mollusks, or shellfish. The shape of a bird's beak can often help you guess what kind of food it eats and where it finds that food. Some birds use their beaks for special tasks. Parrots, for example, use their large and powerful bills to hold on tightly to branches when they are climbing trees. Birds also use their beaks for preening, carrying nesting materials, and making nests.

Beaks for sieving food
Flamingos hold their extraordinary beaks upside down in the water to eat. The lower beak pumps water against filters in the upper beak. These filters sieve out plants and animals for food. Flamingos live around saltwater lakes.

A hummingbird's long, thin beak reaches inside the deepest flowers.

A long reach
Hummingbirds feed on nectar from flowers. These tiny birds use their long, thin beaks and tongues to reach right inside the flowers for their nectar. As they feed, hummingbirds hover in front of a flower by beating their wings very rapidly. Hummingbirds are found in North and South America.

Seed crackers

Finches have short, cone-shaped beaks that are ideal for cracking and crushing. Members of the finch family, such as the goldfinch *(right)*, eat hard seeds, grains, and nuts.

Dabbling for food

Teals are dabbling ducks, which means they use their broad, flat bills to sieve the water for food. Ducks live around ponds and streams and eat small water animals and plants.

FACT BOX

• Hummingbirds can beat their wings at speeds of up to ninety beats per second. They are named for the humming sound made by their beating wings.

• Birds have no teeth with which to break up their food. Plant matter is ground up in a muscular stomach chamber called the gizzard. Some birds swallow small stones and grit, which helps break down food in the stomach.

A falcon's hooked beak is ideal for tearing food.

Tool for tearing

Peregrine falcons are birds of prey. They use their hooked beaks to tear food into pieces small enough to swallow.

FEEDING BIRDS

EEDING birds is one of the best ways to get these cautious creatures to come close enough to study. Whether you have a garden or just a windowsill, you can easily put out scraps of food or a homemade suet cake. Birds appreciate these tidbits, particularly in cold or snowy weather. Better still, build a birdfeeder and put out birdseed, bread crumbs, and bits of cheese and fruit. Be sure the food you put out is not spoiled or moldy. Spoiled food will harm the birds. Watch the birds that visit your birdfeeder. How many different kinds come to eat? Which species prefer each kind of food? Write down the date, time, and weather conditions whenever you see a new species. Do many birds of a species come to feed? Do the birds feed quietly together, or do they fight over scraps?

M A T E R I A L S

You will need: lard or fat, bowl, spoon, unsalted chopped nuts, oatmeal, bread crumbs, string, scissors, plastic cup.

Hang your suet cake on a tree branch or from a windowsill. Watch to see what kinds of birds feed from it.

Make a suet cake

1 Soften the lard or fat. (Ask an adult to help you melt it in a saucepan.) In a bowl, combine the nuts, oatmeal, and bread crumbs. Add the fat and stir well.

2 Cut a long piece of string. Tie a big knot at one end. Put the string into a cup so the knotted end is at the bottom. Spoon the mixture into the cup and pack it down.

3 Refrigerate the suet mixture until it is firm. Pull the string gently to remove the cake from the cup.

MATERIALS

You will need: two 10-inch (25-centimeter) and two 6-inch (15-cm) strips of wood, 8- x 12-inch (20- x 30-cm) piece of plywood, glue, hammer, small nails, paintbrush, varnish, 4 eye hooks, scissors, string.

Build a birdfeeder

1 Lay wood strips along the edges of a piece of plywood (*as shown*). Glue them into position.

WARNING
Ask an adult to supervise you. Do not put out salted nuts. They harm birds by dehydrating them.

2 When the glue is dry, turn the plywood over. Hammer nails through it into the strips of wood.

3 Varnish the top surface of the board to make it waterproof. When the varnish is completely dry, turn the board over and varnish the bottom, too.

4 Screw an eye hook into a wood strip at each corner. Cut two pieces of string, each about 12 inches (30 cm) long. Tie the string to the eye hooks (*as shown*).

5 Hang the birdfeeder from a tree by placing the strings over a strong branch. Adjust the strings until the birdfeeder hangs evenly.

HUNTING BIRDS

Nighttime hunter
Owls have excellent eyesight, which makes them good night hunters. Some owls have flat, disk-shaped areas on their faces that help direct sound into their ears. An owl's ears are at the sides of its head; they are not the tufts on top of the head.

Abird's senses are perfectly suited to search for the particular food it eats. The most important senses for birds are sight and hearing. Different kinds of birds have perfected their own ways to find food. Birds of prey, such as hawks and eagles, have keen eyesight. They can spot mice, rabbits, and other small mammals from a great height and dive down to seize them in their claws. These birds hunt by day. As daylight fades, birds that hunt at night, or nocturnal hunters, such as owls, take over. Other species, including crows and magpies, are scavengers that are always on the lookout for a meal. They eat anything they can find, from worms and seeds to live animals, dead animals, called carrion, and the eggs of other birds.

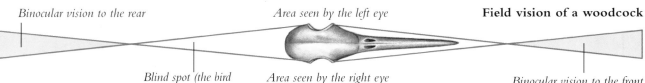

Binocular vision to the rear

Area seen by the left eye

Field vision of a woodcock

Blind spot (the bird can see nothing here)

Area seen by the right eye

Binocular vision to the front

All-seeing eyes
A woodcock *(below)* eats earthworms and insects, so it does not have to spot prey like an owl does, but it must keep a lookout for enemies. Its eyes are on the sides of its head *(above)*, which means it can see all around itself.

Keen eyes
Owls and other hunting birds have forward binocular vision. Binocular vision is sight that uses both eyes. The eyes face forward and focus on the subject *(right)*. Binocular vision makes owls experts at judging distances.

Field vision of an owl

Area seen by the left eye

Binocular vision (area both eyes see working together)

Area seen by the right eye

Large eyes see in great detail and judge distance well

Carrion feeder

A vulture is a scavenger. It eats carrion, which is the flesh of dead animals. Its head and neck are bare, so it can eat without feathers getting into its food. Lappet-faced vultures *(above)* feed in a group.

Silent flier

A barn owl *(above)* swoops down on its prey. Owls have excellent hearing. They can hear the smallest squeaks or rustles made by prey at night. In many species, the ears are on different levels to help the bird pinpoint the exact direction of sounds. The barn owl's feathers have finely fringed edges that allow it to fly almost silently, ready to attack its prey without giving itself away.

Diving for food

Brown pelicans *(right)* dive to eat. Their pouchlike bills are excellent nets for scooping up fish. Other pelicans hunt in groups. They circle around a school of fish to drive the prey toward the waiting beaks of the other birds. Pelicans live on lakes and seas.

SIGNS OF FEEDING

B IRDS eat a variety of foods and feed in different ways. As they peck at nuts, fruits, and berries, their beaks leave telltale marks. Signs like these can help you identify the birds that made them. Become a bird detective by searching for leftovers from bird feasts. A good field guide will help you determine whether food remains were left by birds or by small animals, such as mice and squirrels. Hunting birds, such as owls and kestrels, leave behind special food remains. These predators swallow mice, and even small birds, whole. Once or twice a day, the bird coughs up, in a tightly packed ball, what it cannot digest. These balls are called pellets. If you examine a pellet closely, you will be able to tell exactly what kind of prey the bird caught and ate.

Look around the bases of trees for all kinds of interesting animal remains. Pellets left by hunting birds can be found under trees with low branches, where the birds might have perched.

Finding food remains

1 Look for nutshells gnawed by animals. Squirrels and mice leave holes and teeth marks. Birds leave peck marks and jagged edges, or they crack nuts in half.

2 Fruit is an important food for many birds, particularly in winter. Garden birds, such as thrushes and blackbirds, peck at apples, leaving large, irregular holes.

3 Song thrushes eat snails. They smash the shell against a stone. (The stone is called the thrush's anvil.) You might be lucky and find the remains of a shell beside a stone.

MATERIALS

You will need: rubber gloves, owl pellet, bowl, warm water, liquid soap, tweezers, paper towel, small box, tissue paper.

Dissecting an owl pellet

1 Wear rubber gloves for this project. Soak the owl pellet in a bowl of warm water. Add a little liquid soap to the water.

2 Gently pull the pellet apart with tweezers. Inside, you will find fur, teeth, and the skulls and bones of small animals.

WARNING
Wear rubber gloves, and always wash your hands after handling pellets and other food remains.

This owl pellet contained the remains of several mice, including skulls, jawbones, and leg bones. It also contained small stones swallowed by the owl to help with digestion.

3 Separate the bones from the fur. Wash the bones in water and pat them dry with a paper towel.

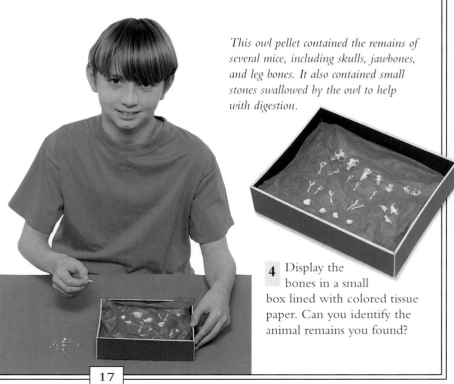

4 Display the bones in a small box lined with colored tissue paper. Can you identify the animal remains you found?

ALL KINDS OF FEET

DIFFERENT birds have feet of different shapes and sizes. Like their beaks, birds' feet are suited to particular lifestyles and habitats. Many birds have four toes on each foot; some have less. Perching birds, as the name suggests, have feet designed for perching. Birds of prey use their feet to catch the animals they eat. They have long, curving claws, called talons, for seizing and tearing at prey. Some waterbirds, such as ducks and geese, have webbed feet that act as powerful paddles to help the birds swim against strong currents in streams and rivers. Wading birds have long toes that spread their body weight over a wider area to prevent them from sinking into the soft mud in which they wade and stand.

Tree climber
A green woodpecker uses its sharp, powerful beak like a drill to get at insects underneath the bark of a tree. Woodpeckers have special feet. Each foot has two toes that point forward and two that point backward. This arrangement helps the bird climb trees and keep a firm grip on the tree trunk while it bores into it for food.

Lily trotter
A jacana is a wading bird that lives in tropical regions. It has very long toes. Because the jacana can step on lily leaves and other water plants without sinking, it is sometimes called a lily trotter.

Champion swimmer

Ducks have webbed feet and spend their lives on or near water. The webbed shape helps them swim efficiently. It also makes them walk with a waddling movement on land.

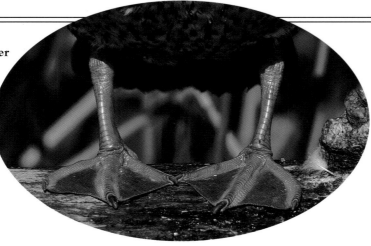

Locking on tight

Perching birds, such as the greenfinch (*below*), have three toes pointing forward and one toe pointing backward so they can lock their feet around twigs and branches. They can perch safely, without danger of slipping, even when they are asleep.

A greenfinch's toes lock tightly around a branch.

Fish catcher

Ospreys have hooked claws that are ideal for catching and holding slippery fish — but make walking a little difficult. Ospreys can be found around seas and lakes in many parts of the world.

LOOKING AT TRACKS

Birds leave many clues to show their presence, even when they cannot be seen. Bird tracks are an important clue. They show the size of the bird that made them and might also tell you to what group of birds it belongs. For example, the tracks left by a duck's webbed feet are nothing like the tracks left by songbirds. Different kinds of birds move in different ways, depending on body size and the shape of their feet. Large, heavy birds, such as geese, waddle along, shifting their weight from side to side. Their tracks show that they often place one foot in front of the other and to the side, somewhat like people do. Small birds, such as chickadees and finches, hop along on thin legs and feet. They leave tracks of tiny prints running side by side. Find some bird tracks and try making casts of the most interesting footprints.

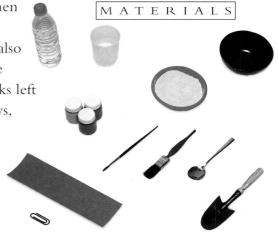

You will need: paper clip, strip of cardboard, bowl, plaster of Paris, water, spoon, trowel or knife, paintbrushes, poster paints.

Make a footprint cast

1 When you are bird-watching, look for tracks in wet sand or mud. Tracks are particularly clear after it has been raining.

2 Use a paper clip to hold the ends of a strip of cardboard together. Press the cardboard ring down gently around a bird's footprint.

3 In a bowl, mix plaster of Paris with water. Add the water gradually and stir well. The mixture should be thick and not too runny.

4 Pour the plaster mixture into the cardboard ring. Let it dry for 15 to 20 minutes. Then, pry up the plaster cast with a trowel or knife.

5 After 24 hours, the cast will be completely dry. Use a soft paintbrush to clean off the soil and grass clinging to the plaster.

6 Decorate your cast with brightly colored poster paints. Use a field guide to help you identify the bird that made the footprint.

WARNING
Always wear gloves when you work with soil.

Learning from tracks
Study the tracks you find very carefully. What do they tell you about the way the bird that made them moves — did it hop, run, or waddle? Think about where you found the tracks and use a field guide to look for birds that live in that habitat. Which bird do you think made the tracks?

These tracks (left) were found in the mud beside a pond. They were made by moorhens.

Moorhens have long toes to help them walk on mud.

FEATHERS

ALL birds have feathers made of a strong, flexible substance called keratin. Keratin is also found in human hair, fingernails, and toenails. Most birds have over 1,000 feathers, many more in winter. Swans have up to 25,000 feathers. Birds use feathers to fly, and feathers keep birds warm and dry. Some male birds use their brightly colored feathers to attract a mate or to warn off rival males. The color of plumage also helps hide some birds from their predators. A hunting bird's feathers often conceal it from its prey. Feathers become damaged during everyday life, so, at least once a year, birds molt — their feathers fall out and are replaced by new ones. During molting time, many birds are more open to attack from predators because they cannot fly as well. Some birds cannot fly at all, even though they have feathers.

Losing feathers
The ragged feathers of this shoveler duck show that it is molting. Some birds molt gradually. Ducks lose all their flight feathers at the same time, so they cannot fly for a while.

Feather types
There are three main types of feathers: wispy down feathers; body, or contour, feathers; and long, slender flight feathers.

Light, fluffy down feathers lie under the contour feathers, next to the bird's skin. They help keep the bird warm.

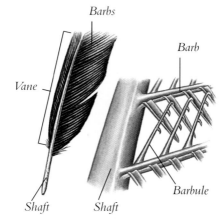

Barbs

Barb

Vane

Shaft

Shaft

Barbule

A feather has thin strands called barbs attached to a central shaft. Each barb of a flight feather has tinier strands, called barbules. Barbules have fringed edges that hook the barbs together, creating a smooth surface that pushes hard against the air.

Contour feathers cover the bird's body. They protect the body and streamline its shape.

Flight feathers are found on the bird's wings and tail. Strong, stiff wing feathers are used for flying. Tail feathers help with steering and braking.

Look at all these feathers. Which ones do you think might be effective as camouflage?

Feathers as camouflage

This plover *(right)*, sitting on its nest among beach pebbles, is difficult to see. Many birds have brown, gray, or mottled feathers to help them blend in, or camouflage, with their surroundings. Camouflage plumage makes the bird's outline less distinct.

Attracting a mate

Male and female mallard ducks have different plumage. The male *(on the left)* uses his brightly colored plumage to attract the female. The female's dull colors help her hide from predators while she sits on her nest protecting her eggs. Male and female birds of many species have different plumage. The feathers of the males are usually brighter.

FUN WITH FEATHERS

EATHERS are fascinating. They are amazingly strong, but weigh almost nothing. They are windproof, and most of them are waterproof, too. Flying puts a tremendous strain on feathers, so birds must work hard to keep them in good condition. Preening cleans feathers and links together the barbs that have split apart. When preening, a bird runs its beak along each feather to smooth it out and to remove any parasites. A bird also uses its beak to oil its feathers. It gets the oil from a special gland near its tail. To resist parasites, birds also take dust baths and bathe regularly in water. You can help the birds in your area by building a birdbath for them in your yard or garden. Keep track of the different species that visit to drink and take a bath.

You will need: rubber gloves, trowel, old trash can lid or large dish, stones, bucket of water.

Build a birdbath

1 Wear rubber gloves and use a trowel to dig a hole in the earth just big enough for a trash can lid or a large dish.

2 Place the lid in the hole and press it down firmly. Be sure it is flat. Put a few large stones into the lid. Birds will use the stones to get in and out of the birdbath.

3 Pour 4 to 6 inches (10 to 15 cm) of water into the birdbath. The tops of the stones should stick out above the water so birds can see them and land on them easily.

Identifying feathers
When you find feathers on the ground, write down when and where you found them in a special book. Use a field guide to identify the birds to which they belong.

To mount the feathers, cut slits in the pages of your book and slide the feathers into the slits. Mounting them this way makes the feathers easy to remove.

Find out about feathers

1 Study a flight feather under a magnifying glass. Split apart the feather's barbs to see the fringed edges, or barbules.

You will need: feathers, magnifying glass, water, tempera paint, paintbrush.

2 Repair the feather's surface the way a bird does when it is preening. Smooth the barbs between your finger and thumb to hook them back together properly.

3 Now, add a little water to some tempera paint and brush the paint onto a feather. Does the paint stick to the feather? What happens? Why do you think this happens?

FLIGHT

THERE are more birds in the world than any other kind of warm-blooded animal. The key to their numbers is flight. Flying allows birds to escape from their enemies and find safe places to perch and sleep. It also helps them find sources of food beyond the reach of most other animals. A bird in flight uses powerful muscles to flap its wings. As the wings flap up, the flight feathers separate to let air pass through. As they flap down, the feathers close and push against the air, moving the bird along. The curved shape of the wing creates lift, allowing the bird to rise in the air. Some birds are in the air for months — or even years. Swifts spend the first three years of their lives in the air, landing only to nest and mate.

A kestrel (above) hovers as it looks for prey. To hang like this in the air, it flies directly into the wind and beats its wings quickly. Some other birds also are able to hover.

Takeoff
This European robin *(right)* was photographed in a special way to get all the stages of takeoff in one picture. When small birds, such as robins, take off, they first leap into the air, then drive their outstretched wings down with a strong stroke. Larger birds must run to gain enough speed for takeoff.

Lift

A bird's wing is slightly curved on top and flatter underneath. This shape is called an airfoil. As a bird flies, the airfoil shape makes air move faster over the wing than under it, creating lower air pressure above the wing and higher air pressure, called lift, below it. Lift makes the bird rise. Aircraft are able to fly because their wings have the same airfoil shape as birds' wings *(illustrated below)*.

Swallows feed in the air. The curved wings and forked tails of these speedy fliers help them maneuver well. They can change direction quickly and catch insects as they fly along.

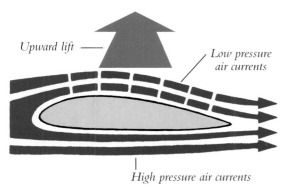

Upward lift

Low pressure air currents

High pressure air currents

An airplane's wing

Curved on top

A bird's wing

Flight patterns

Different species of birds fly in different ways *(right)*. Their flight patterns can help identify them, even when they are just tiny specks in the distance. Small birds, such as finches, make a dipping movement as they fly. Large birds, such as ducks and geese, fly straight and at an even height.

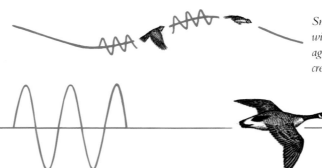

Small birds flap their wings and then fold them against their bodies to create a dipping pattern.

Large birds flap their wings almost constantly to maintain an even course.

FLYING MODELS

You will need: scissors, paper, glue, pencil, needle, embroidery cotton.

Fᴌʏɪɴɢ has many advantages for birds, but it also has an important disadvantage — it takes a lot of energy. Hovering uses the most energy. Many birds are able to save energy in flight by gliding on air currents. Seabirds, such as albatrosses, glide for long distances on ocean air currents without having to flap their wings. On land, warm air currents, called thermals, spiral upward in columns. Large birds of prey, such as hawks, soar in these currents, with their broad wings stretched out to trap as much air as possible. Make your own airfoil to find out how the shape of a wing produces lift. Then, make a soaring spiral to see how birds circle in warm air currents.

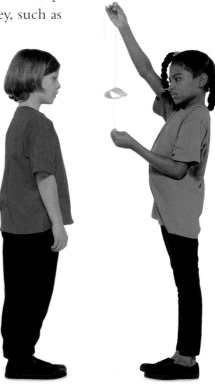

Make an airfoil

1 Cut a strip of paper, 12 x 3 inches (30 x 7.5 cm). Glue the short ends together. After the glue dries, bend the paper into an airfoil shape (curved top, flat underneath).

2 Mark the center of the airfoil. Thread a needle with a long piece of embroidery cotton and push it through the center mark. Pull the airfoil down the thread.

3 Ask a friend to hold the thread taut. Blow hard against the curved edge of the airfoil and watch the wing climb up the thread.

You will need: compass, construction paper, colored pencils or felt-tip pens, scissors, pencil cap eraser, pencil, spool of thread, pin, thimble.

Make a soaring spiral

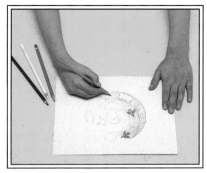

1 Use a compass to draw a large circle on construction paper. Then draw and color in a spiral with hawks flying around it.

2 Carefully cut out the decorated spiral and make the hole left by the compass in the center of it a little bigger.

3 Put a pencil cap eraser over one end of a pencil; put the other end into a spool of thread. Stick a pin into the top of the eraser. Place the enlarged hole in the center of the spiral over the eraser so it is sitting right on top of it. Balance the thimble on top of the pin.

Your model must be well-balanced to work properly.

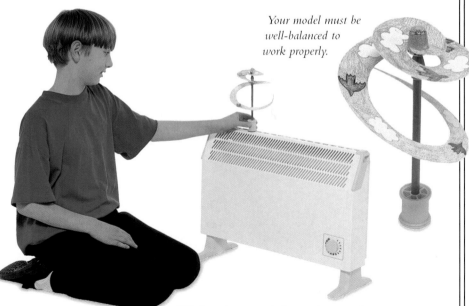

4 Stand your spiral on a heat register or radiator and watch the hawks circle around in the warm air currents.

FLIGHTLESS BIRDS

I N prehistoric times, many kinds of flightless birds roamed the earth. Only a few families, mostly in the Southern Hemisphere, are still alive today. Some flightless birds live on islands where they have few natural predators. To make up for the fact that they cannot fly, most flightless species are strong runners or swimmers. Ostriches, rheas, and emus are too large and heavy to fly, but they can run very fast to escape danger. Other species, such as penguins and flightless cormorants, are expert swimmers and divers. Many flightless species have died out. The dodo and the giant moa of New Zealand have become extinct in the last few hundred years.

Island dwellers
Cormorants are seabirds. Most kinds of cormorants are good fliers, but a species that cannot fly lives on the Galápagos Islands, off the coast of South America. This species has survived because there are no predators on these remote islands that hunt cormorants for food.

Wingless bird
The kiwi is a flightless bird from New Zealand that has no visible wings or tail. It is a ground-dwelling bird that hunts for food at night. The kiwi depends on its sense of smell to locate earthworms and insects in the soil. Its long, slender beak has sensitive nostrils near the tip.

Ocean hunters

Penguins *(left)* are flightless birds of the Antarctic. They are superb swimmers and divers with wings that act as flippers to propel them along. Penguins are graceful in water but clumsy on land. Sometimes they slide over the ice using their chests as toboggans!

Outrunning danger

The African ostrich *(below)* is the world's largest bird. Ostriches can run at high speeds, escaping most predators. They live in grasslands that are usually dry, but where sudden rains can cause heavy floods. So ostriches can also swim.

The extinct dodo

Dodos were heavy birds that lived on islands in the Indian Ocean. Sailors hunted them for food, and, by 1800, the last dodos had been wiped out.

FACT BOX

• The emperor penguin dives to depths of 290 yards (265 m) to search for fish. It can stay underwater for up to twenty minutes.

• Able to swim 25 miles (40 kilometers) per hour, the magellan flightless steamer duck from South America is the fastest-swimming duck.

• A bird known as the island rail lives on the remote island of Tristan da Cunha in the Atlantic Ocean. The island rail is the smallest flightless bird in the world. It is only 5 inches (12.5 cm) long, about the same size as a hen chick.

MIGRATION

Formation flying
Snow geese make long journeys, or migrate, in groups. They fly in *V*-shaped formations or long chains. Young birds learn the route by following the older birds in front of them. In contrast, swallows find their migration route by instinct.

MANY kinds of birds travel great distances each year to escape the chill of winter or to find food or a safe nesting site. Some of these journeys cover thousands of miles (km). Departure is often triggered by the shorter daylight hours of early autumn. In spring, the birds travel back again, often returning to within a few miles (km) of their original starting point. These incredible journeys are called migrations. Many species do not feed while they travel, so they must fatten up before they leave. Migrating birds face many hardships and dangers. They can get lost in storms or be killed by predators. Before each trip is over, thousands of birds die of hunger, thirst, and exhaustion.

Fattening up
The American golden plover *(above)* migrates from North America to South America. In autumn, it eats large quantities of insects and shellfish to fatten up for the long trip. Birds that do not migrate also fatten up in autumn to survive the long, hard winter.

Migrant champion
The arctic tern *(below)* is the long-distance champion of the animal kingdom. Each year it travels from the arctic region to Antarctica and back again, a round trip of 22,370 miles (36,000 km). The tern takes advantage of the long daylight hours of summer in each region to eat well before moving on again.

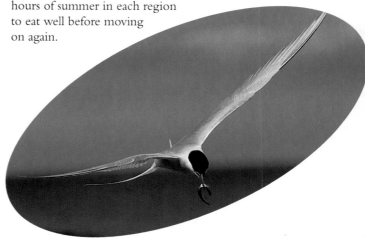

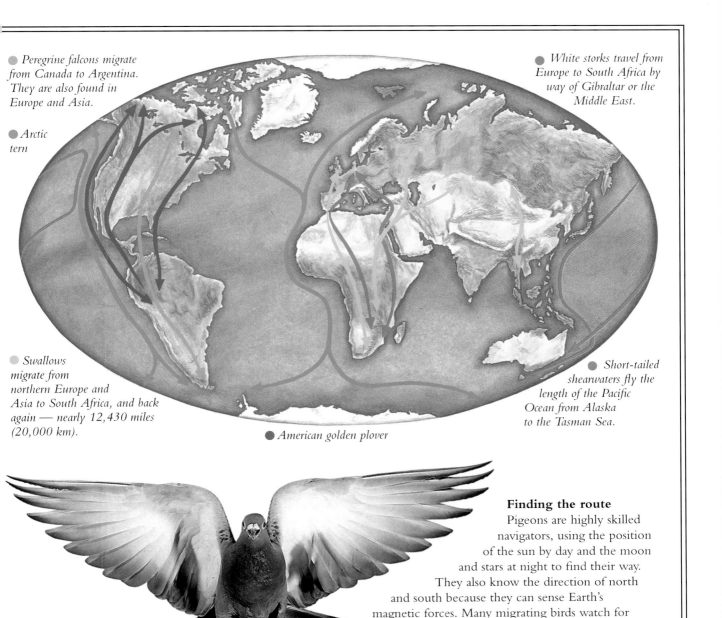

● Peregrine falcons migrate from Canada to Argentina. They are also found in Europe and Asia.

● Arctic tern

● White storks travel from Europe to South Africa by way of Gibraltar or the Middle East.

● Swallows migrate from northern Europe and Asia to South Africa, and back again — nearly 12,430 miles (20,000 km).

● American golden plover

● Short-tailed shearwaters fly the length of the Pacific Ocean from Alaska to the Tasman Sea.

Finding the route
Pigeons are highly skilled navigators, using the position of the sun by day and the moon and stars at night to find their way. They also know the direction of north and south because they can sense Earth's magnetic forces. Many migrating birds watch for familiar landmarks, such as mountains and lakes.

CALLS AND SONGS

THE sound of singing birds is music to most people's ears. Yet the songs that seem so beautiful to us are mostly aggressive in meaning. They are sung by male birds to establish their territories. A territory is a patch of ground where birds intend to breed or feed. A bird's call or song identifies both its species and itself as an individual. In Antarctica, a parent penguin finds its chick among thousands of other chicks by its cry. Birds also call to warn of danger and to attract a mate. Birds that flock together use contact calls to stay in a tight group. For example, the honking cries of flying geese help the group stay together during their migration.

Sounding the alarm

A female European blackbird makes a harsh clacking sound to warn other European blackbirds of danger, such as approaching cats or humans. Small, flocking birds often make this kind of alarm call to members of their group. The bird sounding the alarm hides from the predator among leaves and branches.

Singing in flight

The male bobolink sings to establish its territory. It sometimes sings from perches. Like the European lark, however, it is more likely to sing in flight as it hovers high above the ground. The bobolink is a small bird found across the open grasslands of North America.

FACT BOX

• The African gray parrot can learn up to 800 words. Most species of parrots can learn only 50 words.

• Starlings are good mimics. They can imitate the sound of a telephone.

• Many birds, including starlings, sing notes too high for human ears to hear.

• Bellbirds make a sound like a bell being struck. They can be found in Central and South America.

Local accent

Birds sing by instinct, but young birds learn a particular song and dialect from their parents. They also learn from other adult birds living nearby. So a chiffchaff *(right)* living in one valley will sing a different song than a chiffchaff living in the next valley.

Identifying call

Gannets *(above)* are seabirds that breed in large, crowded colonies on cliff ledges. While she is rearing her young, the female gannet stays on the nest. The male bird hunts for fish. When the male returns to the nest, he has to find his mate among thousands of other birds, so he calls to his mate and identifies her by her answering cry.

Natural mimics

Parrots, such as these macaws *(left)*, are good mimics, which means they have a natural ability to imitate all kinds of sounds, including human speech. This talent has made these colorful birds of the tropical rain forests popular as caged birds. This talent, unfortunately, also has threatened the survival of some kinds of parrots.

LISTENING TO BIRD SONGS

When you go out to listen to or record bird songs, don't go alone. Take an adult with you. When you hear a new song, write down exactly what it sounds like, so you will remember it later.

Lⁱˢᵗᵉⁿⁱⁿᵍ to bird songs is a good way to identify different kinds of birds. Even when a bird is hidden in long grass or leaves, you can recognize it by its unique song. Species such as the American robin and the scarlet tanager look similar, yet they have uniquely different songs. The best times of day to listen to birds are dawn (the dawn chorus) and dusk, when birds sing loudest. You can have a lot of fun recording different bird songs. Use a portable tape recorder with a long microphone cord, so you can position the microphone away from your hiding place. Tape the microphone to a stick, so the sound of your hands on it will not be recorded. Headphones let you hear what you are recording. For better results, make a sound reflector out of an old umbrella.

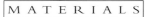

Tape some bird songs

You will need: portable tape recorder (with a microphone, a long microphone cord, and, if possible, headphones), blank cassette tapes, notebook, pencil, waterproof mat or cushion.

1 Become familiar with the songs of birds that live in your area by listening to recordings on CDs or cassette tapes borrowed from your local library. After you complete this project, you can listen to your own bird tapes!

2 Outside, hide behind a tree or a bush, if possible. Set up the microphone near a birdfeeder or near a perch where you see a bird singing.

3 Use the record and pause buttons on the tape recorder. Release the pause button when you want to record. Listen with headphones, if you have them.

4 Write down the time, place, and weather conditions for each song you hear. When you listen to the recordings at home, use a field guide to identify the birds that are singing.

Make a sound reflector

1 Cover the inside of an old umbrella with foil. Bend the foil over the edges of the umbrella and tape it down securely.

MATERIALS

You will need: old umbrella, aluminum foil, tape, tape recorder (with microphone and headphones), blank cassette tape.

2 With the head of the microphone pointing toward the foil, tape the microphone to the stem of the umbrella, 6 to 8 inches (15 to 20 cm) away from the shade.

3 Set up the reflector where birds are singing. It will channel sounds and make them louder, or amplify them. Give the birds time to get used to this strange object.

COURTSHIP AND BREEDING

Displaying plumage
A male peacock *(above)* fans out his beautiful tail feathers to attract a female peahen. He wants to show her that he is fit to father healthy offspring. Some male birds of other species also display their colorful feathers to attract mates.

For a bird species to survive, the birds must find mates and breed. Birds are, by nature, cautious of each other, but they overcome this wariness by courting. Courting involves making special signals before mating, with the male birds usually attracting the females in some way. In many species, the males' brightly colored plumage attracts their mates. Some male birds court females with special rituals. They might offer food to show they can provide well for the young, or they might put on displays of singing or dancing. Some species pair only briefly to mate — the males usually mate with a number of females in one year. Other species pair for the whole breeding season and raise their young together. Some species, such as golden eagles, swans, and gannets, pair for life.

FACT BOX

• It seems that, in general, most female birds prefer to mate with older, more experienced males, rather than with younger birds.

• Flamingos pair for a lifetime. Some stay with their mates for fifty years or more.

• The female spotted sandpiper courts the male. She lays her eggs in the male's nest and leaves them for him to keep warm, or incubate, until they hatch. She goes off to find another mate.

Dancing ground
Sage grouse are ground-dwelling birds of North America. The males court the females by staging dance displays. They fight to win patches of ground, called leks, that are used just for dancing. Females gather around the leks to watch the dancing. Then they mate with the best dancers.

Inflated pouch

To attract a female, the male frigate bird *(below)* puffs out the bright red pouch under his chin. The pouch inflates like a balloon and can stay puffed up for several hours. A female chooses the most impressive bird to mate with and signals her choice by rubbing her head against that male's pouch.

Water dancers

Great-crested grebes *(above)* often pair for life. Males and females court by performing complicated dances on the water. There are four separate dances. Performances last several weeks before the two birds mate and raise a family together. These birds are found on freshwater lakes.

Bower builder

The male Australian bowerbird *(right)* courts females by building a beautiful shelter called a bower. Different species of bowerbirds build bowers of different shapes. Some are shaped like towers and others even have corridors. The male often decorates his bower by arranging brightly colored objects around it. Male bowerbirds might mate with several females in the bower. After mating, the females build their own nests to raise their young.

BIRDS' NESTS

Nests are warm, safe places where birds lay their eggs and where young birds, or nestlings, develop after they hatch. Nests are not homes where birds sleep at night. To sleep, birds roost on perches in sheltered places, such as hedges and trees. Nests vary greatly in size and design. Some are simple scrapes in the ground; others are quite elaborate. The first step in nest building is choosing a good site. Then the birds gather building materials, such as grass, twigs, leaves, feathers, moss, wool, and mud. Constructing the nest is usually the female's job. She pushes the materials into place and hollows out the inside with her body. The finished nest might be lined with soft materials, such as feathers.

This puffin has gathered some dry grass to line its nest. Birds build nests from whatever materials they can find. The puffin digs a nest burrow in a grassy cliff top by scraping out the earth with its beak and pushing the soil away with its feet.

Hollowed out
A thrush's nest is made of grass and twigs. It has a hollow inside where the eggs will be safe and warm. To make the hollow, the female bird turns around and around in the center of the nest, pressing down on the grasses with her breast.

Thrush nest made of grass and twigs

Inner hollow shaped by female

Outer cup shape

Hanging basket

Weaverbirds *(below)* from Africa build very elaborate nests. These birds can tie knots in grass with their beaks and feet. They use this skill to make a loop of grass, suspended from a twig. They add more grass to form a hollow chamber. The nest might be round, bell-shaped, or oval. Some kinds of weaverbirds add an entrance tunnel to protect the nest from snakes that might steal the eggs.

Pinewood home

This hummingbird *(left),* known as Anna's hummingbird, has built its nest on a pinecone. Hummingbirds are very tiny, and they build extremely small nests. Some of their nests are no bigger than a Ping-Pong ball.

Stork nest made of sticks and branches

Rooftop site

White storks *(right)* build enormous nests on top of roofs and chimneys. They also use natural sites, such as cliffs and trees, for their nests. The nests are usually made of sticks and branches. Storks are found in various parts of Europe, Asia, and Africa.

NESTING BOXES

Nesting birds are fascinating to watch. You can attract birds into your yard and help them nest and raise their young by building a nesting box. Not all birds like nesting boxes, but many common birds do. The box shown in this project will attract small perching birds. Spring is nesting season for birds, so it is the best time to set up your box. During this busy time, you might see birds fly by, with nesting materials in their beaks, looking for a place to build. Many birds wedge their nests in the forks of tree branches. Nest building takes a lot of time — a week, or even a month — yet most nests last only one breeding season and then are ruined by winter weather.

Left diagram measurements:

← 6 inches (15 cm) →

8 inches (20 cm) — *Roof*

12 inches (30 cm) — *Back*

4 inches (10 cm) — *Front*

8 inches (20 cm) — *Side*

7 inches (17.5 cm) — *Side*

6 inches (15 cm) — *Base*

← 4½ inches (11.2 cm) →

← 8 inches (20 cm) → ← 7 inches (17.5 cm) →

Use pine or plywood, ½ inch (1.2 cm) thick. Ask an adult to cut these pieces (above).

MATERIALS

You will need: pieces of wood (cut by an adult to the sizes shown at left), wood glue, small nails or tacks, hammer, pencil, strip of burlap (for a hinge), varnish, paintbrush.

Build a nesting box

1 Arrange the pieces of wood in place to be sure they fit together properly. Glue the front of the box to the base. Let the glue dry.

2 Carefully glue one of the side pieces into place. Let the glue dry.

3 Glue on the other side piece. After the glue dries, nail these pieces together. Center the box on the back piece and draw around it.

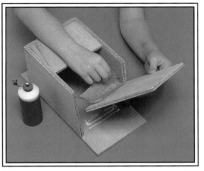

4 Following this guideline, nail the back piece to the box. Add the roof piece by gluing and nailing on the burlap hinge.

5 The nesting box will last longer if you varnish it, inside and out. Let the varnish dry overnight.

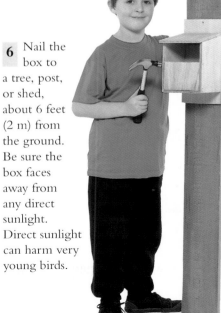

6 Nail the box to a tree, post, or shed, about 6 feet (2 m) from the ground. Be sure the box faces away from any direct sunlight. Direct sunlight can harm very young birds.

When you are nailing the box together, tap each nail into the wood, just a little ways, with the wood flat on your work surface. Then, hold the wood in position to drive the nail in completely.

WARNING
Never frighten nesting birds. Do not go close to nests while they have eggs or nestlings in them. Never touch any bird's eggs.

Nesting materials
In spring, hang some nesting materials, such as wool, string, grass, moss, or feathers, from branches or a windowsill. You could also set out tissue paper, straw, or animal hair. Different bird species like different materials. Watch to see which materials the various birds choose.

BIRDS' EGGS

ALL birds reproduce by laying eggs. To keep them safe from predators, most eggs are camouflaged with colors that blend in with their surroundings. The size of birds' eggs varies dramatically among species. An ostrich egg is thousands of times heavier than a hummingbird egg. The number of eggs laid also varies. Small birds, such as warblers, lay up to a dozen eggs. Some larger birds, such as albatrosses, lay only one. In most species, the female bird sits on the eggs to warm them with her body while young birds develop inside their protective eggshells. The process of development, called incubation, might take weeks — or several months. Some types of cuckoos' eggs hatch in just ten days, but the eggs of the wandering albatross take nearly three months to hatch.

Well-hidden
The eggs of this little ringed plover are camouflaged to blend in with pebbles on the beach. This camouflage makes it extremely hard for predators, such as gulls, to see them.

Investigating eggs
Find out more about eggs by looking at a hen's egg. Remove a piece of shell from the less pointed end of the egg *(right)*. What do you see? Carefully crack the egg into a dish *(left)*. The yellow yolk is a young bird's food supply. The transparent albumen supplies vitamins and water.

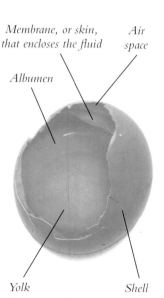

Membrane, or skin, that encloses the fluid

Air space

Albumen

Yolk

Shell

One clutch or more?

The blue tit lays just one clutch, or batch, of ten to twelve eggs in the spring. Some birds lay more than one clutch. When the blue tit's eggs hatch, the nestlings are fed caterpillars, which are in good supply at that time of the year. Blue tits are found in Europe, North Africa, and Southwest Asia.

Special designs

The murre is a seabird that lays its eggs on cliff ledges, which seems like a dangerous place to lay eggs. A murre's eggs, however, are pointed at one end. If the egg is bumped, it rolls around in a circle, without falling off the ledge.

A special shape keeps the egg from falling off the cliff's ledge.

During a single summer, the female European blackbird lays three clutches of up to four eggs each, so there will be enough food for all the nestlings. The nestlings eat worms, which can be found all year round. European blackbirds live in parts of Europe, North Africa, South and West Asia, and New Zealand.

YOUNG BIRDS

A hatching baby bird can take hours, or even days, to break through its shell. The young bird pecks its way out using the hard, bony tip on its beak, called the egg tooth. The newborn chicks of birds, such as ducks, that nest at ground level are well developed and have a covering of feathers. Their eyes open almost immediately, and they can stand after an hour or so. Mallard chicks can swim and feed themselves only hours after hatching. In contrast, the chicks of birds that nest in trees are weak and helpless. The parent birds are busy all day bringing food to their hungry nestlings. Blue tit parents must find ten thousand caterpillars and a million aphids to raise their brood. Fueled by enormous amounts of food, the nestlings develop quickly. After two to three weeks, they are ready for their first flight.

Newly hatched European blackbirds are blind and have no feathers. They are totally dependent on their parents for the first two weeks of life. They open their mouths wide and cheep to beg for food.

A hatching chick

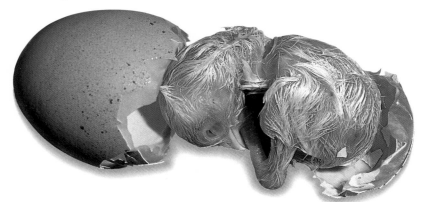

When a hen chick hatches from the protective covering of the egg, it first punches a circle of holes near the less pointed end of the egg. Then, it pushes off the top of the eggshell with its head. The chick struggles until it is completely free of the shell, then rests to recover its strength. When it first hatches, its feathers are still damp and waxy from being inside the egg.

After only twelve hours, the chick's feathers are completely dry and fluffy, and the chick is strong enough to stand up properly and move around.

First flight

A young wren *(below)* is clumsy when it first attempts flight. At about sixteen days old, the feathers of a wren nestling are fully grown, so it prepares to leave the nest. Yet, the nestling is still dependent on its parents and follows them around, begging for food. By copying the actions of adult birds, nestlings soon learn the skills they will need to take care of themselves.

Caring fathers

Male emus *(above)* and ostriches are good fathers. They mate with several females, who all lay their eggs in the father's nest. When the chicks are born, the male cares for them and raises them. He uses his body to shade them from the fierce heat of the sun.

FACT BOX

• Some birds are heaviest when they are young. A wandering albatross nestling, for example, can weigh as much as 43 pounds (19.5 kilograms). It takes ten and a half months to raise an albatross chick.

• Hoatzin chicks live in the Amazon rain forest. They leave the nest long before they can fly. Special claws on the edges of their wings help them climb trees.

• The chicks of large bird species often take the longest to hatch. Emu chicks take sixty days to hatch. Small songbirds take only about two weeks.

Following mother

This duckling *(above)* has recognized a beagle as its mother, because the dog was the first animal the duckling saw after hatching. This behavior, called imprinting, is a natural instinct of ducklings.

WOODLAND BIRDS

Woods and forests are ideal homes for birds. They can fly up into tree branches to escape from ground-dwelling predators. In summer, leaves hide them from sight completely. Many birds roost and nest in trees. Trees also provide nesting materials and food. A wide variety of insects live in trees and lay their eggs in the bark. The eggs hatch into grubs and caterpillars that stay on the trees to feed on leaves. The birds, in turn, eat these small creatures. Both birds and insects are the most plentiful in woods of deciduous broad-leaved trees, which are trees that lose their leaves in autumn. Owls, pigeons, cuckoos, jays, thrushes, woodpeckers, and warblers all live in these trees. In Europe and North America, oaks are the favorite trees of many birds. Fewer bird species live in evergreen forests, but mixed forests of broad-leaved trees and conifers are quite popular.

Waxwings are found in evergreen forests. They live in flocks and feed on insects and berries. When food is very scarce during winter, large flocks migrate to new areas in search of a meal.

Nighttime singer

The nightingale is a shy bird that lives in the woods and scrublands of Europe, Asia, and Africa. Its brown plumage keeps it hidden, but its beautiful song is unmistakable. Male nightingales sing to establish breeding territories. Nightingales are famous for their nighttime singing, but they also sing by day.

FACT BOX

• A green woodpecker eats as many as two thousand ants each day.

• The ivory-billed woodpecker was once common in the woods of the southeastern United States. Now, it is one of the world's rarest birds.

• During the winter of 1965-66, more than 11,000 waxwings made the journey from Siberia and Finland to Britain in search of food. The winter weather was particularly harsh in Siberia that year, and very little food was available.

Crossed beak

Crossbills *(left)* live in the pine forests of Scandinavia, Britain, and the United States. Their only food is pinecone seeds. Their unusual, overlapping beak is designed to tear open pinecones to reach the seeds.

Nutcracker

A nuthatch *(left)* wedges a nut into a crack in tree bark to hold the nut firm while it pecks the nut open with its sharp beak. Nuthatches are found in the woodlands of Europe and North America. They eat berries as well as nuts.

Woodland drummer

Woodpeckers *(right)* are woodland birds that nest in dead and dying trees. They chisel holes in tree trunks with their strong beaks and build their nests in the holes. Woodpeckers also use their beaks to drum on tree trunks to establish their territories and to warn others to stay away. Many kinds of woodpeckers can be found in Europe and North America.

WOODLAND BIRD-WATCHING

You will need: 8 short poles, string, scissors, 6 long poles, canvas or tarp, safety pins, 4 tent stakes, leaves and twigs.

Birds are easiest to see in the woods during the winter months as they busily hop among the bare branches in search of food. In the spring and summer, the leaves of the trees provide dense cover for birds, so it is much easier to hear them than to see them. In spring, many birds sing loudly to establish their breeding territories. You might also hear a sudden burst of drumming as a woodpecker drills out a hole for its nest. By late spring and summer, you might hear the cheeping of young birds demanding food from their parents. Look for birds near ponds and streams, where they gather to drink and bathe. Wherever you decide to look, bird-watching in the woods will be much easier if you build a hiding place, called a blind. Remember, always take an adult with you on your woodland trips.

Build a blind

1 With a friend to help you, lay four short poles on the ground in a square. Tie the ends together with string. Repeat these steps to make another square.

2 Have your friend stand inside one of the squares, holding the other one in position for the roof, while you tie four long poles to each corner of the base and roof.

3 Strengthen the structure by adding two long poles placed diagonally across opposite sides of the blind. Tie them to opposite corners of the base and roof.

4 Cover the sides with canvas, adding a small piece for the roof. Fasten all canvas edges with safety pins. For extra stability, anchor the base to the ground with tent stakes.

5 Attach some leaves and twigs to the canvas covering of the blind for camouflage, to make it blend in with the woods and be less obvious to the birds.

6 From inside the blind, you can look out through the openings between the safety pins. If you have them, use binoculars. Be still and quiet, and birds will soon approach.

Tepee blind
A tepee is another, simpler kind of blind. You will need four to six poles, string, a tarp, safety pins and, possibly, tent stakes. Fan out the poles to form a pyramid shape and tie the top ends together with string. Drape the tarp around the poles and fasten it with safety pins.

Camouflage the tepee with leaves and twigs. Leave an opening in the cover to look through with your binoculars.

FRESHWATER BIRDS

Some birds spend their lives on or near fresh water — rivers, lakes, and ponds. Their bodies are designed for aquatic living. For example: ducks have broad bodies and webbed feet for swimming, swans have long necks for feeding underwater, storks and herons have stiltlike legs for standing in water and long beaks for spearing fish. Different species prefer to live at various places along a river's course. Upstream, near the river's source, dippers and wagtails hop among the rocks of fast-flowing streams. Kingfishers, ducks, and grebes live on rivers and by the still waters of lakes and ponds. As a river nears the sea, it flows more slowly and widens into an estuary, where tides send currents of saltwater swirling upstream twice a day. Wading birds, such as sandpipers and plovers, feed there.

This common loon (above) is wearing its winter plumage. Loons are skilled swimmers. They plunge under the water to catch fish with their sharp beaks. This small family of birds has only four species.

Paddling along
Moorhens live by still or slow-flowing waters and streams. They dive underwater to search for food. Their long toes have unusual flaps of skin that spread out, when the bird swims, to push against the water. The flaps close as the foot is brought back in again.

FACT BOX

• Bewick swans have bright yellow beaks with black markings. Each bird can be identified by its beak, because each bird has a different beak marking.

• In 1990, chemicals spilled into a river near Norwich, in eastern Britain, causing swans living on the river to turn a bright blue color. Fortunately, the swans did not seem to be harmed in any way.

• When danger threatens the chicks of the jacana, the parent bird tucks the babies under its wing and carries them to safety.

Skillful swans

This mute swan *(left)* is coming in for a landing. Taking off and landing on water is very difficult, but ducks and swans are experts. To land, the swan spreads its wings to slow down and uses its feet as brakes when it hits the water. To take off, the swan beats its powerful wings and runs along the surface of the water until it gains enough speed and lift to leave the water.

Upturned bill

Avocets are birds of seashores and river estuaries. They have long, slender beaks that curve upward at the end. As the avocet wades in shallow water, it sweeps its beak from side to side to catch worms and shellfish.

Keen eyesight

A kingfisher *(right)* is an expert at catching fish. A parent bird has to catch large quantities of fish to feed its young. It presents the fish headfirst, so they are easier to swallow. This bird's eyesight is excellent. As it skims above the surface of the water or perches on an overhanging branch, it can spot fish under the water.

WATCHING WATERBIRDS

Dᴜᴄᴋs, swans, and geese are familiar sights on lakes and ponds. These birds belong to the same order, which has 150 species worldwide. Bird experts divide ducks into two groups — dabblers and diving ducks. Dabblers, such as mallards and teals, feed on or just below the water's surface. Some upend their bodies as they feed, so just their tails are showing above the water. Diving ducks, such as tufted ducks, feed in deeper water farther out. They dive down to feed on the bottom and disappear for some time before bobbing up again. Some diving ducks pop back up in the same spot. Grebes and other diving ducks reappear in different places. Watch some waterbirds and make notes about their habits. Approach them quietly, or you will frighten them away.

Staying down
Don't hide behind a bank, wall, or hedge where your head will be outlined against the sky when you raise it to peek over. Hide behind a bush or clump of reeds that you can look through instead of over.

Approaching birds
Test the wind direction by wetting your finger and holding it up in the air. Approach birds downwind, so that the wind is blowing from the birds toward you. When you are downwind, the sounds you make are less likely to be heard by the birds.

Getting close
As you get closer to a bird, crouch down and move steadily forward. Birds will probably notice you less when you move directly toward them, rather than moving sideways.

54

You will need: field guide, stopwatch (or watch with a second hand), notebook and drawing pad, pen and pencils.

Looking at diving birds

1 Choose a pond or lake for bird-watching. See where different species feed. Notice where they dive and reappear. Use a field guide to help you identify species.

2 Find out how long different birds stay underwater. Use a stopwatch to time their dives. Do they eat underwater, or bring their food to the surface?

3 Record the times in your notebook. Which bird stays underwater the longest? Do you think the length of time is affected by the depth of the water?

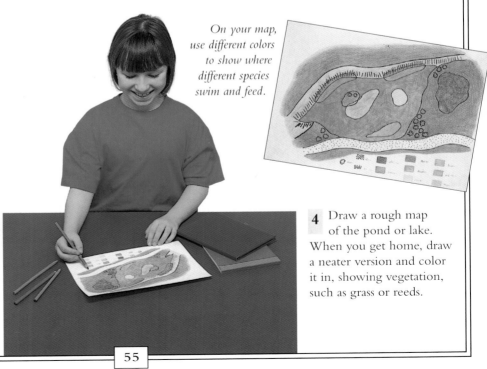

On your map, use different colors to show where different species swim and feed.

4 Draw a rough map of the pond or lake. When you get home, draw a neater version and color it in, showing vegetation, such as grass or reeds.

BIRDS OF SEAS AND SHORES

SEAS and oceans cover more than two-thirds of Earth's surface, yet only a small proportion of the bird kingdom is seabirds. Conditions are very harsh on the seas, even though there are plenty of fish and other sea creatures to eat. Seabirds, such as terns and albatrosses, ride the winds over the open ocean, thousands of miles (km) from land, but they must return to land to breed. Their cliff-top colonies are almost deserted in winter, but, in spring, every rocky ledge is lined with birds. Many kinds of birds can be found on seashores around the world. Different species prefer different seashore habitats, from salt marshes and mud flats to sandbanks and rocky shores.

Safety in numbers
Oystercatchers are wading birds. They feast on shellfish and mussels found on rocky shores. The size of their flocks protects them from predators, such as peregrine falcons. A falcon can be confused by the large mass of birds and miss them all.

Identity bands
Scientists studying birds and their movements often use numbered bands to identify individual birds. The bands are usually made of metal and are attached to the birds' legs. When a bird is found, its band shows how old it is and how far it has flown. If you find a band, it might have a phone number to call or an address where you can send it.

Double camouflage
The colors of the sooty tern's plumage provide two kinds of camouflage. The tern is dark on top, so predators, such as gulls, circling above it find it hard to spot the bird. Its belly is white, so when the tern hunts fish in the water below it, the fish cannot easily see the bird above.

Ocean wanderer

Albatrosses *(left)* are found, for the most part, south of the equator. These birds soar in the air currents above rolling ocean waves. Albatrosses glide effortlessly and can cover distances of up to 560 miles (900 km) a day.

Rare visitor

Shearwaters *(below)* roam the oceans, migrating great distances each year. They come to land only to breed. When on land, their legs are weak, so they are very wary of predators. Males visit their mates in the nest only at night, under cover of darkness.

Crowded colonies

Murres *(right)* nest in pairs on crowded cliff ledges. Each pair has a tiny territory, just big enough to incubate one egg. Fighting in such tightly packed colonies would injure many birds and eggs, so these birds use a language of threatening and nonthreatening movements to resolve arguments before any fights break out.

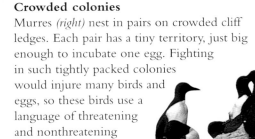

BIRDS OF REMOTE PLACES

Birds of the world's mountains, tundras, and deserts are specially adapted to survive in these harsh, bleak places. Mountains and tundras have short, cool summers and long, icy winters. They have high rainfall or snowfall and howling winds. Their main advantage is that few people go there, which makes them a refuge for some bird species that have been driven out by humans elsewhere. Few birds, except eagles, live on mountaintops, where there is little to eat. Grouse and small songbirds, such as buntings, are found on the tundra below. They eat berries, seeds, and heather shoots. Golden plovers and curlews visit these remote places to breed but migrate to the lowlands to avoid winter weather. Deserts are harsh places, too, with scorching heat and little food. The birds living there also must find special ways to survive.

Ptarmigan in winter

The ptarmigan is a well-known bird of the arctic tundra. Its plumage changes with the seasons to blend in with its surroundings. In autumn, the ptarmigan molts and grows a winter coat. The new plumage is white to blend in with the winter snow.

Ptarmigan in summer

In summer, the ptarmigan's feathers are brown to blend in with the heather. Grouse, pheasants, and ptarmigan are called game birds because hunters shoot them for sport at certain times of the year. Many people strongly oppose this practice.

Desert runner

Roadrunners live in the dry desert regions of Central and North America. They rarely fly but can run fast to catch snakes and lizards. They sometimes kill their prey by dashing them against rocks. The roadrunner avoids the searing desert heat by staying in the shade until dusk.

Mountain predator

Some eagles are fierce hunters of mountain regions. They soar high above crags and hillsides, searching for rabbits, small rodents, and grouse. When an eagle comes upon an unlucky victim, it swoops down and seizes the prey in its claws.

Grouse are ground-dwelling birds of forests and grasslands in Europe, Asia, and North America. These hardy birds also live in the arctic tundra.

RAIN FOREST BIRDS

ABOUT two-thirds of all bird species live in the world's rain forests, near the equator. Rain forest birds are often brightly colored, with markings that blend in with the forests' exotic flowers and dense foliage. Some rain forest species, such as parrots, have short wings that make it easier for them to fly among the branches. The tall trees of the rain forest, many of them evergreen, provide good roosts and nesting sites. They also provide leaves, fruits, flowers, and plenty of insects for the birds to eat. Unfortunately, large areas of rain forest have been cleared to make way for mining operations, new roads and villages, and grazing land for cattle. As the forests are cut down or burned, many bird species are becoming endangered or at risk of dying out completely. Sadly, scientists only recently have discovered some of the birds at risk.

Oversized beak
Colorful toucans live in the Amazon rain forest. They have enormous beaks that they use to reach for fruits on branches too thin and light to hold the bird's weight.

FACT BOX

• The toco toucan is the largest toucan. Its bright orange bill is 8 inches (20 cm) long — one-third of its total body length.

• The harpy eagle comes from the rain forests along the Amazon River in South America. It is one of the largest eagles in the world. This fierce hunter preys on monkeys.

• In tropical forests, hummingbirds drink up to eight times their weight in water every day.

King of the bush
The kookaburra is, perhaps, the best-known bird in Australia. It lives mainly in the drier areas around the edge of Australia's rain forests. The kookaburra has a very noisy cry that is often heard in towns at daybreak. It calls at this time to proclaim its territory.

Nectar feeders

Some sunbirds *(left)* live in tropical forests. With their long, slender beaks, they can reach right inside tropical flowers to sip nectar.

Sacred bird

Quetzals *(right)* live in the rain forests of Central America. Male quetzals have bright red breasts and the longest tails of any bird. Long ago, their tail feathers were prized by Mayan and Aztec people who worshiped the quetzal as a god.

Hard-headed bird

The hornbill *(right)* is named after the horny ridge, called a casque, on top of its head. Hornbills nest in trees, as woodpeckers do. The male bird seals up the nest opening to keep the female inside while she incubates the eggs. He feeds her through a narrow slit.

CONSERVATION

MANY kinds of birds flourish around the world. In the last fifty years, however, certain species have become increasingly rare. Some are now in danger of extinction. The survival of these birds is threatened in many ways. Their homes might be destroyed as forests are cut down. They might live in wild country where marshes and grasslands are being cultivated. Species, such as birds of paradise from Southeast Asia, are being hunted for their beautiful feathers. Kestrels and other birds of prey are sometimes poisoned by chemical pesticides that have been absorbed by the small animals they feed on. Some predators are considered pests and are shot by farmers. Oil spills and pollution threaten seabirds. Fortunately, more and more people are becoming aware of these problems and are joining the fight to save the world's birds.

There are many ways to help with bird conservation, from putting up a nesting box to properly disposing of litter. Cut up the plastic loops that link aluminum cans. Birds can get tangled in them and, possibly, choke. Contact your school or library to find out about bird-watching or nature clubs to join.

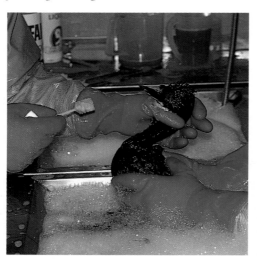

Saving birds

Conservationists are cleaning a scoter *(left)* whose feathers are clogged with oil. Rescuing birds from oil spills at sea is just one of the important jobs of the bird conservation groups that exist in many countries. They set up reserves to keep birds safe, work to preserve birds' habitats, and campaign against pollution.

FACT BOX

• The Japanese crested ibis is one of the rarest birds in the world. Probably fewer than fifty crested ibises are alive today.

• In 1989, a large oil spill from a tanker called the *Exxon Valdez* polluted approximately 1,180 miles (1,900 km) of coastline in Alaska and killed up to 100,000 seabirds.

• The takahe is a type of rail from New Zealand. It is so shy that, for many years, it was thought to be extinct.

Whooping cranes

Whooping cranes *(above)* once migrated in large numbers from the Gulf of Mexico to the Great Plains of North America, where they bred in lakes and swamps. Their survival was threatened when the swamps were drained for farmland. Now they are protected birds, and their numbers are slowly increasing.

New enemies

The kakapo *(left)*, a flightless parrot from New Zealand, once had few natural predators on the islands. Now, however, animals, such as cats and rats, that have been introduced to New Zealand by humans in the last few hundred years, are preying on kakapo eggs and young.

Out of danger

The nene goose *(left)* is a conservation success story. This goose, which comes from the Pacific islands of Hawaii, was once nearly extinct. Then, a few pairs were brought to a bird reserve in Britain, and they began to breed. Flock numbers gradually increased, and, now, some geese have been released back in Hawaii, and the nene is officially off the list of endangered species.

GLOSSARY

airfoil – a wing-shaped form with a curved upper surface that, when moving through the air, creates an upward push, or lift, underneath to hold it up.

albumen – the clear, thick liquid surrounding the yolk of an egg; the egg white.

barb – a thin, and often stiff, hairlike strand that branches out from the central shaft of a feather.

barbule – a tiny hairlike strand that branches off the barb of a feather and has fringelike hooks that hold the barbs of the feather together to keep air from passing through.

blind – a small, protected or enclosed place outdoors, that usually blends in with the natural surroundings, where a person can hide to watch wildlife in their natural habitats.

bower – a shelter, usually found in a yard or a garden, that is often made out of twigs and vines.

breed – (v) to produce young, or offspring, through the mating of males and females of a species.

brood – a group of young birds that hatched and are being cared for together.

camouflage – coloring, shape, or movement designed to hide something by making it blend in with its surroundings.

carrion – the rotting flesh of dead animals.

clutch – the group of eggs laid by a bird at any one time.

contour feathers – medium-sized feathers shaped to cover the main body, or contour, of a bird.

courting – acting in a way that will attract a partner for mating.

endangered – threatened with serious harm or loss; in danger of extinction.

estuary – a wide place at the lower end of a river where the ocean tide flows in.

extinction – the condition of a species having died out completely and no longer existing.

family – a group of animals within a particular order that have similar behaviors and physical features.

habitat – a place or area with living and growing conditions that are, by nature, suitable for a particular animal or plant.

hatch – to come out of an egg as the offspring of a species.

hover – to hang in midair, over a certain point or area on the ground below, without flying forward, backward, sideways, or around in circles.

imprinting – a learning process occurring very early in an animal's life that forms the behaviors of the animal based on its attraction to others like it or to a substitute.

incubation – the process of sitting on eggs to keep them safe and warm so the young inside them will fully develop and hatch.

lek – a piece of ground, or area, where animals display courtship behaviors.

lift – a force pushing upward, such as the upward push created when an airfoil, or wing, moves through the air.

maneuver – to move and change direction or position with skill or careful planning.

mating – a male and female of a species joining together for the purpose of producing young, or offspring.

migrate – to move from one place to another at regular intervals, usually over very long distances, to find a more suitable place for feeding and breeding.

molt – to shed or lose an outer covering, such as skin, hair, feathers, or shells, before growing a new covering.

nestling – a young bird that has not yet left the nest.

nocturnal – active at night.

order – a large group made up of families of animals that are similar by nature.

perch – (v) to land or rest on something above the ground, such as a branch, post, or wire.

plumage – a bird's entire covering of feathers.

predator – an animal that hunts other animals for food.

preen – to clean, smooth, and tidy the feathers with the beak.

prey – (n) an animal that is hunted by other animals for food.

propel – to push or drive forward with a natural or a mechanical force that creates motion.

ritual – a series of actions designed and performed for a specific purpose; a ceremony.

roost – (n) the place where a bird rests or sleeps; a perch.

scavenger – an animal that feeds on garbage and carrion.

sieve – (v) to pass material through some kind of strainer that separates large pieces from small ones or drains off liquids.

species – a specific group within a family of animals that have many common characteristics and can breed with each other.

talon – the claw of a bird, such as an eagle, that kills and eats other animals for food.

taut – pulled or stretched tight; tense; not loose or relaxed.

thermals – rising currents of warm air over land.

tundra – a large area of flat, treeless land in arctic regions.

wary – watchful and cautious to avoid danger.

yolk – the yellow part of an egg, which is the source of food for the unhatched offspring of birds.

BOOKS

Birds, Birds, Birds! Ranger Rick's Naturescope (series). (Chelsea House)

Birds: Masters of Flight. Secrets of the Animal World (series). Eulalia García (Gareth Stevens)

Birds, Nests, and Eggs. Young Naturalist Field Guides (series). Mel Boring (Gareth Stevens)

The Dodo. The Moa. Extinct Species Collection (series). Tamara Green (Gareth Stevens)

Endangered Birds. Endangered! (series). Bob Burton (Gareth Stevens)

The Great Bird Detective. David M. Elcome (Chronicle Books)

Hawks, Owls, and Other Birds of Prey. Close up: A Focus on Nature (series). Denise Fourie (Silver Burdett)

Penguins. Animal Families (series). Annette Barkhausen and Franz Geiser (Gareth Stevens)

Seabirds. Mark J. Rauzon (Watts)

The Search for the Origin of Birds. Prehistoric Life (series). Lawrence M. Witmer (Watts)

Urban Roosts: Where Birds Nest in the City. Barbara Bash (Little, Brown & Company)

Wings Along the Waterway. Mary B. Brown (Orchard Books)

VIDEOS

Backyard Birds. (National Geographic Society)

Birds, Birds, Birds. (Quality Books)

Birds of Prey in the Natural World. (Educational Activities, Inc.)

Jr. Zoologist: Birds. (United Learning, Inc.)

Understanding Birds (series). Adaptations. Nesting. Behavior. (Nature Episodes)

Wonder Why: Birds. (Lucerne Media)

WEB SITES

www.petersononline.com/birds/perspective/index.html

home.earthlink.net/~pazuzu/orn.html

Some web sites stay current longer than others. For further web sites, use your search engines to locate the following topics: *bird, bird-watching, feather, flight, migration, nesting,* or any individual bird's name.

INDEX

PICTURE CREDITS

b=bottom, t=top, c=center, l=left, r=right

Bruce Coleman Limited: 10b, 11b, 15tr, 16br, 19t, 23bl, 26b, 27t, 30t, 30b, 31c, 34b, 39t, 40t, 41t, 41br, 45tl, 46t, 49b, 57t, 61tr, and 63tl. Frank Lane Picture Agency: 14b. P. N. Johnson/BBC Natural History Unit: 35tr. Mary Evans Picture Library: 31b. Papilio Photographic: cover, 4t, 4b, 5t, 5c, 9tl, 9tr, 9c, 9bl, 9br, 10t, 11tl, 11tr, 14t, 18l, 18r, 19bl, 19br, 21bc, 21br, 22t, 23br, 26t, 32bl, 32br, 34t, 35tl, 35b, 38t, 38b, 39c, 39b, 41bl, 44t, 45tr, 45b, 46bl, 46br, 48t, 48b, 49tl, 49tr, 52t, 52b, 53t, 53bl, 53br, 56t, 56c, 57c, 57b, 58l, 58r, 59bl, 59br, 59t, 60r, 61tl, 61b, 62b, 63tr, and 63b. Warren Photographic: cover and 33b. Zefa Pictures: 5b, 15tl, 15b, 31t, 32t, 47tl, 47tr, 47b, and 60l.